To Dr M. J. Smith,
with thanks ~ C.F.

For Doreen and family,
with love ~ B.C.

SIMON AND SCHUSTER

First published in Great Britain in 2014 by Simon and Schuster UK Ltd
1st Floor, 222 Gray's Inn Road, London WC1X 8HB
A CBS COMPANY

This paperback edition first published 2015

A CIP catalogue record for this book is available from
the British Library upon request

ISBN: 978-1-4711-4405-9 (PB)
ISBN: 978-1-4711-2447-1 (eBook)

Printed in China
3 5 7 9 10 8 6 4 2

Monsters Love Underpants

Claire Freedman & Ben Cort

SIMON AND SCHUSTER
London New York Sydney Toronto New Delhi

Monsters think it's MONSTER fun,
To creep around, all scary!
But there's something they love even MORE,
Than looking mean and hairy!

Monsters all LOVE underpants,
And think pants are fun-tastic.
They like all patterns, shapes and styles,
And twanging pants elastic!

Some prowl through dingy dungeons, "Oooooow!"
You hear them howling, loudly.
CREAK! One finds squeaky armour pants,
And clanks around SO proudly!

Drool monsters from the steamy swamp,
Fill pants with gooey slime.
But, OOOOPS! Their pants get slippery,
And slide down all the time!

Wild, woolly mountain monsters
Make explorers faint with fright!
CLOMP! They snatch their frozen pants,
Then run off in the night!

At the bottom of the ocean,
A pirate ship now rests,
Where sea monsters wear pants with jewels,
They've pinched from treasure chests!

The spiky, spooky, space monsters
All wave and roar, "Hooray!"
When out from blackest, deepest space,
Bright bloomers float their way!

It's not the sand inside his pants
That makes this monster tetchy.
His underpants are way too small,
"I wish they were more stretchy!"

It's Saturday – their Disco Night,
Held in a secret cave.
The password (sshh!) is WOBBLY PANTS!
To get inside the rave.

The monsters show their pants off,
As they dance The Monster Bop.
Their pants-clad bottoms jig and jive,
Till someone yells out "STOP!"

"It's almost daylight! Quick, back home . . .
We can't risk being spotted!
For no one will be scared of us,
In pants all striped and dotted!"

So if you hear strange scuffles
From beneath your bed – beware!
You might just catch a monster,
Trying on YOUR snazzy pair!